MUSIC
MOVES ME
WORSHIP
MOVES GOD

By

D O N N A J . S I M M O N S

Steward Publishing, LTD.
🌐 stewardpublishing.org

DEDICATION

I would like to dedicate this book to the Lord Jesus Christ who gives me the ability to live a life of love in Him. Because of Him, I am.

To my husband, Kurt, who allows me to be all God has called me to be. He supports me in anything and everything I do. From being a man of God, to an excellent father, PawPaw, friend, and my life support. My friend, Katie calls you "The Great Wonder, I call you husband, friend, the wind beneath my wings."

To my family; my village. I have two smart, beautiful daughters, Nikrista and Tiffany. My sons, Ryan and Jordan, and bonus son, Marcus. My daughters in love, Abi, and Janina. Grandchildren, Deondria, Teanna, Andreas, Ryan Elijah, Jacob, Judah, and J'ana. To my crew of five great granddaughters whom I love unconditionally. To Mother Dorothy Smith and my father, Deacon Sam Smith. Thank you for a solid foundation. They taught me how to love God's people and cope with life. To my sisters and brothers. Carolyn (my trailblazer), Sherry (my stabilizer), Sammy, and David (my minstrel, a true David Levite). Alvin and Diana Lindsey (my teachers). Doris Williams, Jackie Shores, Bishop Oney and Susie Fitzpatrick, Joan, and Michelle Walker, who always saw the best in me (aka Angel). Mamma Valeria Harris, all of my aunts, uncles, and cousins. God has been good to me. Michelle Clemens, my prophetess. Joe Huff, the prophet. Mother Bishop Pat McKinstry for your love, support, guidance, and impartation. I can't leave out my prayer partner, friend, devil-slaying armor bearer, Debbie Shumpert. Thank you for pushing me. Uncle Junior. Every girl needs an Uncle Junior, but you can't have mine!

FOREWORD

I met Pastor DJ when she was about 8 years old. It was not a planned meeting but one that God would develop into a lasting friendship and mentorship. I attended service one Saturday night at her home church and upon entering I heard the sweetest little melodious voice. Upon inquiring who the singer was, I was told she was Donna Jean Smith. I said to the person, "she sings like an Angel." I was introduced to her parents, the late Sam and Dorothy Smith. This began a lasting friendship with the entire family that still continues to this day.

I have been given a front row seat in the development of the Holy Spirit taking Pastor DJ from a lead singer and soloist to a worshipper. I have observed how the Holy Spirit began to take her to different levels in prayer and deliverance. Her heart for God and His people opened up the bowels of her compassion causing the heavens to open up and pour down the miraculous. As Pastor DJ elevated in God and accepted her calling to preach, she shifted higher. The Word of God opens us up to enhance our relationship with God deeper and fuller. Our desire to know Him brings us into another dimension of praise and Pastor DJ's voice and worship were eminent to capture her audience and move them and God. Moving in music causes God to move in the atmosphere.

Pastor DJ is a remarkable psalmist, intercessor, and preacher. She is willing to expend herself for the kingdom of God so that we His people may receive all God has for us no matter the setting.

(BISHOP JOAN WALKER)

Introduction

This book has been a long time in the making through experiencing the power of God in the area of worship. Turning our focus off of ourselves and putting our focus on God. You may say "what do you mean?" I'm glad you asked. The songs we sung were about our struggles, our troubles, and sometimes even the Blues. Those songs moved us, and we could relate to them. Those songs would have you all in your emotions; you would be clapping, rocking, and crying but it wasn't edifying God. It was then that I discovered that was not all what God wanted. So, I decided to shift the direction of my praise to focus on God, His name, His power, and His word. For example, I would sing "God don't move my mountain, but give me the strength to climb." I love that song, it moves me because the Bible clearly tells us to speak to the mountain, and God is intentional in His word. Mark 11:23 says, (KJV) "For verily I say unto you, that whosoever shall say unto this mountain "Be thou removed and be cast into the sea, and shall not doubt in his heart, but shall believe that those things which he says shall come to pass. He shall have whatsoever he says."

Worship comes from understanding His love, being touched by His power, and acknowledging Him in the fact of who He is. He responds to His word. He moves when He hears His word. Music moves me. Worship with my music moves God.

CHAPTER 1

My Beginning Stages: A Life of a Worshipper

Hello Reader,

As you are reading this many of you may be thinking, "Another book on worship?" Well, yes, because He is so multifaceted, and this is just my perspective as one of the citizens of the kingdom of God as a worship leader that sings. Before I became a worship leader I was, and still am, a student of prayer. Personally, as a child until I was thirty-three years old, I only served at one church. I attended Sunday School and sung with Mass Youth Choir. Now you had to be seventeen to sing in the adult choir. But, just at the tender age of fifteen God saw fit to elevate my gift and I was placed in the adult choir after a conversation with my mom Mother Dorothy Smith. The rules of the choir said I was not old enough to be in the adult choir, but I was skilled enough, so the pastor allowed it after having a meeting with the Bishop (our

Pastor) the choir director Alvin Lindsey, and my mother. I came from the generation of respect and obedience. If Pastor Bishop, the choir director, or if anyone had not agreed, I would not have been allowed to sing in the adult choir.

A few other mothers received permission for their underage daughters to join the adult choir after me. They were allowed, but that was the beginning of me noticing that like it or not, when there is a called anointing on your life, everything is attracted to you, good and bad. When there is an anointing on your life, attacks will come from all different places: friends, family, coworkers, church members. Your motives are pure, and you don't have to do anything, but can be misunderstood. There is a story in the Bible when Joseph told his brothers his dream. His motives were pure, but they were offended. In Genesis chapter 37 Israel (Jacob, Joseph's father) loved Joseph more than all of his children because he was the son of his old age. He made Joseph a coat of many colors. Verse 4 says, "And when his brethren saw that his father loved him more than all his brethren, they hated him, they could not speak peaceably unto him." Have you ever wondered why some people can't even speak to you? It's because they see the anointing on your life. The story continues that then Joseph dreamed a dream and told his brethren. The details of the dream in verse 6 through 11 say, "for behold we were binding sheaves in the field and lo my sheaf arose and stood upright. And behold your sheafs stood around about and made obeisance to my sheaf. And his brethren said unto him 'shall; though indeed reign over us? Or shall thou indeed have dominion over us?' And they hated him yet the more for his dreams and for his words. And he dreamed yet another dream, and told it his brethren, and said, Behold, I have dreamed a dream more; and, behold, the sun and the moon and the eleven stars made obeisance to me. [10] And he told it to his father, and to his brethren: and his father rebuked him, and said unto him, What is this dream that thou hast dreamed? Shall I and thy mother and thy brethren indeed come to bow down ourselves to thee to the earth? [11] And his brethren envied him; but his father observed the saying." So many things happened due to the anointing and the call on his life. Likewise, the same attacks can come to you. When his father sent him to take food to his brothers, they saw him coming from afar off. Yes! They can see you coming. His brothers announced, "The dreamer is coming. Let's kill him." Your anointing brings haters, plots, schemes, and will be a part of your journey.

My choir days were a great highlight of my life. Boy we could sing! Alvin Lindsey, his wife (Diana), and family were so committed to the music ministry at the church. Although I was underage, my mother allowed me to go with the church family, and I was able to participate in church outings, and traveling with them, but she was definitely hands-on. I had my limits. I loved the choir, I loved to sing. We went many places: Washington, D.C, West Virginia, Tennessee, Kansas. Because I was still in school, Mondays were rough for me. The choir was superb. Pastor Alvin's teaching is still in me today. Parts and tone were very important. He knew just what songs to sing and just who to choose for the leads. My mind is racing through all of the beautiful women of God that touched my life. I watched them in their marriages, being wives and having children, cooking, and keeping their family in church. Our entire church was one big family.

I came from a singing, anointed family (The Ballards). We sang at home and prayed. Church was our life. My oldest sister, Carolyn was a strong alto. I sang soprano. My brother was one of them bad, cool tenors. All of my formative years were at the church. We had a youth choir called the Mass Choir. Ruth Jackie Shores was our director. She was before her time as well as my godmother, Valeria Harris. Her choir was the United Glorious Voices.

In my teen years I developed a love for God and His word. I was filled with the Holy Ghost at 17. From there it was a whirlwind. Years went on and at 21 years old I had my first child. In those days they didn't play. The Bishop sat me down and I was unable to sing with the choir. We also had a group called The Gospel Experience. We went out on a program, and I sang with them. When we returned, I got called into the office. I got the message, no singing while pregnant out of wedlock. I had to answer to everybody. There was a lot of hurt and a lot of disappointment. In 1983, my son was born, and six months later Kurt and I were married. My husband received the Holy Ghost, and we raised our children to love God, family, and the church. I also became a bonus mom to my two daughters. They were eight and eleven when we married. By the time they were eleven and fourteen they came to live with us. Home, school, and church was our life. Our second child Jordan was born. Sports came into the picture. Kurt and I both worked a lot of hours. I owned my own beauty salon. There were many family reunions and bus trips. Our lives were full. Our family was strong, and the church was strong.

Then the Word became a love for me. Many Evangelists would come to the church and preach. Our church, Glorious Apostolic, was on fire full of young folks. Some of the young people would disappear when it was time for the word. Mamma had that eye on me, so I had to stay in the building. I started listening. Then I started to fall in love with the stories about David, the Praiser who loved the Lord and who was after His own heart. I asked one of my minister friends, Michelle Walker aka Tini, where the stories about David were at in the Bible. She said, "Start in First Samuel." I found him and could not put it down! I started reading the Bible like a harlequin romance. I was intrigued. I had to get a dictionary to look up words like "garrison" and "rent in his clothes." I wanted to understand every word!

Growing up, what do you remember that changed your perspective about God? Take some time to jot down your thoughts.

_____

_____

_____

_____

_____

_____

_____

_____

_____

_____

_____

_____

_____

_____

_____

_____

_____

_____

_____

_____

_____

_____

_____

_____

_____

_____

_____

_____

_____

_____

_____

_____

C H A P T E R   2

The Study Began with the Love of the Word

Father teach me to be a student of Your word. I pray in every situation I face; I look to You for guidance, Your word says, "Seek and you will find." I thank You that Your word is spirit and light. I can call on You and You will answer in the name of Jesus.

There are going to be some scriptures that you will never fully understand until you go through some circumstances in your life. That makes it come alive for you.

Rhema Word. The Rhema Word can happen when you're reading a particular passage of scripture. Perhaps one you have seen many times before and you now see it in a new light and see how it applies to your life personally. The word of God is what God answers to. It's like your words that you speak out of your mouth. You know what you said and if you are integral, you can and will back your words up. If I said it, good or bad, I have to recognize it and back it up. I learned to pray the answer instead of the problem. When you are in trouble or sick, pray the word. Pray the solution. I once heard, "Don't tell God your problems, but tell your problems about God."

In the beginning was the word, and the word was with God, and the word was God (John 1:1). I believe that praying scripture is powerful. We are holding God to His word. We are confessing our will to His will. "So is my Word goes out from my mouth it will not return to me empty, but will accomplish what I desire and achieve the purpose for which I sent it" (Isaiah 55:11).

Sometimes life can hit you so hard. You lose a loved one, then many loved ones very close to each other. I was a caregiver for my beautiful mother who was diagnosed with dementia. I would call it "Heaven's Language" because it got to the point sometimes, she didn't know who I was. It was unbearable at first until it hit me! Wow, I believe that's how Heaven will be. We will feel and know love by the spirit, not by the flesh. Come on, imagine with me. Mother would respond to love, care, and compassion. Her loved ones no longer had names, but instead personalities. I had to come to terms with her soft touch, hug, and smile without the full knowledge of her knowing who I was. Husbands won't know wives or children. We will all be brothers and sisters, sons, and daughters. We will all be children of God. Can you imagine that?

Okay, let me elaborate a little bit on my theory of this. Me being a woman that lost two husbands by death, then I die. Which one would I choose because I loved them both during my time on Earth while I was alive? I'm telling you now, we are not taking all that Earthly stuff into eternity. 1 Corinthians 15:42 NIV says

"So also is the resurrection of the dead. It is sewn in corruption, but it is raised in incorruption. 43 It is sewn in dishonor; it is raised in glory: it is sewn in weakness, it is raised in power. 44 It is sewn a natural body, it is raised a spiritual body. There is a natural body, and there is a spiritual body. And so it is written, the first Adam was made a living soul; 45 the last Adam was made a quickening spirit. 46 Howbeit that was not first which is spiritual, but that which is natural and afterward that which is spiritual. 47 The first man is Earthly, the second man is of the Lord from heaven. 48 As is the Earthly such are they also that are Earthly. And as is the heavenly such are they also that are heavenly. 49 And as we have born the image of the Earthly we shall also bear the image of the heavenly. 50 Now this I say brethren, that flesh and blood cannot inherit the kingdom of God; neither does corruption inherit incorruption. 51 Behold I show you a mystery, we shall not all sleep, but we shall all be changed. 53 For this corruption must put on incorruption and this mortal must put on immortality."

I can recall when being in church when it came time for the preached word, it would bore me and didn't get my attention until they would tune up (when the musicians would come behind the preacher with music, if you were a singer, it would be runs). They would make it exciting! I would wait for the scripture, the subject, and that fancy good 'ole topic. Sometimes it would be a relatable catch phrase like Iona Locke preaching a message called "Let's Get It On." Bishop Jake preached "Stay In The House" and "Woman Thou Art Loosed." These are some of the ones you may have heard. I've heard at least a thousand more, I have some pretty good ones myself. It was so exciting. We would get all worked up running, and shouting. It felt so good! We stomped the devil, turned around three times, made a giant step forward, and danced. The music and the whole experience was great! But, like the scripture says, "And some fell on stony ground, where it had not much earth; and immediately it sprang up, because it had no depth of earth; but when the sun was up (when things got hot) it was scorched; because it had no roots, it withered away". Soon as you left the church, things started to fall apart. Even before you could get out of the parking lot, "Sister Sandpaper" said something to upset you, or "Little Johnny" got jacked up by the mean boy. You know what I mean. Not taking anything away from the message of the preached word. It's that the enemy came to take the Word away. And some fell on thorns, and the thorns grew up, and choked it, and it yielded no fruit. (Mark 4:7). An example of that is reading your Bible on your cell phone without putting it on Do Not Disturb. Then texts come in and you're distracted by Facebook, Tik Tok and Instagram. Before you know it, you've wandered off. These devices can be Word-thieves. You're so distracted you've missed the Word. The Bible talks about "good ground", that yielded forth fruit, "that sprang up with increase and brought forth some fruit some thirty, some sixty, some one hundred fold."

Well, let's talk about the shift of being a hundredaire in the word. Can you say, "Word of faith movement?" Bibles, pens, pencils, and notebooks came to church. We would hold up our Bible and say Joel Osteen's quote, "This is my Bible. I am what it says I am. I have what it says I have. I can do what it says I can do." It was all about the word. We had a revival at our church, Glorious Apostolic with Creflo Dollar Jr. Honey, it was a game changer. Prayer, praise and worship, an opportunity to give, and then the word. What? No choir? If that wasn't enough, I came one night and sat down by my favorite Word-Girl. We would get the word and commentary, slap five, nudge each other when they hit a bullet point. Honey, Pastor Dollar paused and said, "Stop all that slapping five, talking and sharing. Hold your thoughts and listen." Yup, scolded by the teacher. Funny now, but it wasn't then, I still like him. I took the correction, got my notebook, and became a student of the word. We were so blessed by the teaching that we would love to study and hear the word.

In a lot of situations I began to face; I took the teaching of going to the word for every situation in life. Scriptures for healing, forgiveness, love, marriage, family, children, finances, and everything in between. Everything that pertains to life is in the word of God. If you are sick, go to the doctor, but heal yourself with the word of God. Find every healing scripture in the word of God and read it out loud. Write it down and meditate on the healing scriptures. Speak the word of God out of your mouth and affirmations according to the word. Partner with His word concerning you, over your body, your family. The Word has the answer for any relationship. My cousin, Pastor Ballard, taught us study is worship. What does the word say about it? I experienced many situations I've had to put the word on. The word will heal your broken heart and your emotions. You can't be lazy. You have to search that word and let the word do the work. If you work the word, it will work for you. "IVE SEEN TOO MANY MIRACLES TO LET DEFEAT HAVE THE LAST WORD", is a song by the Williams Brothers, which I personally know to be true.

I was introduced to seven Hebrew words of praise. All the ways you praise God brings worship to Him like the clapping of the hands, and dancing as an example. The Hallal, Yadah, Barah, Tehillah, Zamar, the Todah, Shabach. Let me take some time to give you the definitions of the seven words.

The first one is Hallal. The Hallal is used 99 times in the Old Testament; more than any of the other words. It is translated as "praise." The word Hallal means "to boast loud," "to celebrate," "to be clamorously foolish." Yes, Hallelujah! A high praise unto God and to God's holy name. When you see someone jumping and running around the church, excited and running with joy, it is a Hallal praise.

The Yadah is the second most frequently translated praise. The word means "to worship with extended hands." To throw out the hands to give thanks to God. Lift up your hands in the sanctuary and bless the Lord (Psalms 34:2). The psalmist declares in Psalms 65:4, "I will lift up my hands in Your name." First Timothy 2:8, "I will therefore that men pray everywhere lifting up holy hands without wrath and doubting." Invoke yourself to praise, arms open and hands extended, giving God praise. Our hands are an inevitable part of almost every response pattern. They are a means of extending, as well as expressing our emotions. Our hands give us a way as no other part of the body, they are an extension of our personalities (The Hallelujah Factor Book). I've been told that raising one's hands is an international sign of surrender.

Then we have the Barak, which means "to bless," or "blessings from God." It means "to kneal," "to bless," "to salute." To praise the Lord, to Barak Him, honor and bless the Lord.

The Tehillah is to sing. It involves music, especially singing. Singing has always been vital in the worship of God. Tehillah is to sing out of one's self in the spirit. How else can I express that? It's singing songs unto the Lord.

The next one is the Zamar. Zamar is "to pluck the strings of the instrument." It's another musical word and is largely involved in joyful expressions of praise. Psalms 150 says "Praise ye the Lord. Praise God in his sanctuary: praise him in the firmament of his power. 2 Praise him for his mighty acts: praise him according to his excellent greatness. 3 Praise him with the sound of the trumpet: praise him with the psaltery and harp. 4 Praise him with the timbrel and dance: praise him with stringed instruments and organs. 5 Praise him upon the loud cymbals: praise him upon the high sounding cymbals. 6 Let every thing that hath breath praise the Lord. Praise ye the Lord."

The Todah. Todah is a word used in connection with an offering and can be taken to mean "to extend one's hands in a sacrifice of praise." It is a thanksgiving or a thanks offering. This praise is connected to faith. You can give a Todah praise and may not see your victory yet. A Todah is thanking Him in advance. I don't see it yet, but I give You a Todah praise.

Then we have the Shabach. This word means "to shout," "to express in a loud tone." Growing up in church we always said it meant to sustain in a loud holler. This is the particular word for shout. We always said "we shouted" which pertains to the dance, but actually this pertains to the Shabach. Shabach is a sound.

We have been demonstrating these words all along, but after study and getting understanding, the actions that follow the words caused the presence of the Lord to show up and His glory is obvious. The glory of the Lord will fill the house. We would dance, shout, run, and cry! The love of God would cover us like a cloud. Time would seem to stand still as the glory of the Lord would take over. I began to teach on the seven Hebrew words of praise in worship seminars and workshops, helping many people to have a greater understanding as to why we do what we do. Let's give praise unto the Lord.

Let's expound in some practical teaching. Write down ways to demonstrate each type of praise. What experiences have you had when using each method?

HALLAL

YADAH

_____

_____

_____

_____

_____

_____

_____

_____

_____

_____

_____

_____

_____

_____

BARAK

TAHILLAH

ZAMAR

TODAH

SHABACH

_____

_____

_____

_____

_____

_____

_____

_____

_____

_____

_____

_____

_____

_____

C H A P T E R 3

Experiencing the Power of Prayer

Prayer should be the lifestyle of a believer. A person who prays daily, prays the word, and has a sanctified set apart, consecrated life. A Prayer Warrior is not just a hearer of the word, but a doer. Confess your thoughts one to another and pray one for another that ye may be healed. The effectual, fervent prayer of a righteous man availeth much (James 5:16). I call that a consecrated prayer life. A consecrated lifestyle sets you apart.

Every type of religion prays. Some do it out of obligation. Some do it hit or miss. Let's look at an Obligation Prayer rather than a Fervent Prayer. James 4:3 KJV says you can pray amiss. "Ye ask and receive not because you ask amiss upon your lust." Now let me say it again out of the Amplified Bible, "You ask God for something and you do not receive it because you ask with wrong motives out of selfishness or with an unrighteous agenda so that when you get what you want, you may spend it on your own desires."

Consecrate means to set apart or being worthy of veneration by association with God, or to keep for a special purpose. Some other definitions mean to bless, hollow, commit, entrust, apply, and bestow. Being set apart and set aside.

Here are some examples of consecrated prayers. Daniel prayed religiously, but fervently (Daniel 6:10-28). The presidents and princes sought to find an occasion against Daniel concerning the kingdom, but they could not find an occasion nor a fault. For as much as he was faithful, neither was there any error found in him. So, they established a plot and spoke to the king words he wanted or needed to hear that would stroke his ego. Watch out for the flesh. The king signed a decree that would entrap Daniel in his prayer life, stating no one could pray for 30 days. If they did, they would be cast into the den of lions.

The enemy will come for your prayer life when it is fervent. Daniel 6:9 says, "Wherefore King Darius signed the writing and the decree." Daniel knew the writing was signed. He went into his house with his window open and his chamber towards Jerusalem. He kneeled upon his knees three times a day and prayed and gave thanks before his God as he did before the decree as signed. He did things as usual. They used the law against Daniel. His prayer life got him thrown into the lion's den. Your prayer life can get you unwanted attention. You will hit targets in your prayer life but, be aware you will also be targeted.

It saddened the king's heart after he realized what he had done. Yes, Daniel's prayer life put him in the lion's den because he was a man of fervent prayer. The lions did not devour him. Daniel received victory! That morning when the King went to the lion's den and Daniel was still alive, the King's report was "Daniel's God is God!"

I used Daniel, but I know you have an experience that you know prayer changed it for you. Take a few moments to remember and jot it down.

_____

_____

_____

_____

_____

_____

_____

_____

_____

_____

_____

_____

_____

_____

The fervent prayers of the righteous availeth much.

Thirty days without prayer is too long. Stay consistent and persistent in your prayer. It can be best practice to have a specific prayer time daily. For example, praying first thing in the morning or at noon. A set prayer time works. Make it a lifestyle.

Your fervent prayer life brings forth much fruit. Be sincere in your prayers. The more fervent you pray, the more confident you will be in knowing God hears and answers your prayers. "And this is the confidence we have in Him. If we ask anything according to His will, he hears us" (1 John 5:14). It continues to say in verse 15 "and if we know that He hears whatsoever we ask, we know that we have the petition that we desire of Him." I use the word when praying because He watches over his word to perform it in our lives. Prayer is worship.

I always loved the women of God having a noon day prayer. They were strong, powerful people. People would seek them out to pray for them. Growing up, they call themselves "The Prayer Band." When you were sick, you wanted them to pray for you. If you had a court case, you wanted them to pray for you. If you had problems in your home, you wanted them to pray for you because their prayers reached heaven.

God placed it on my heart to have a 9 o'clock prayer at our church, Glorious Apostolic. It was confirmed by our first lady, Susie Fitzpatrick. God moved in a powerful way. One day a young man with an unclean spirit showed up. He was attracted to that prayer time at the church. He started to act out. About the same time God sent a brother from Nigeria, Africa who was drawn to pray with us every morning. He was a blessing. He taught us how to war in the spirit in prayer. As we interceded and prayed, he cast the unclean spirit out of the young man. That was a powerful experience. We were glad he was there. He taught us the importance of our part in interceding for him as he was in warfare. That is a very powerful combination. We have to cover ourselves and one another and do it strategically. Every day we would end with holding hands and praying together in a circle. The anointing and power of God would be so strong, when one of the other ministers and I would embrace we would both fall out in the spirit. Honey, you talking about drunk in the spirit! It was Pentecost every morning. God moved mightily! Word got out that 9 o'clock prayer was going on and many began to come. When visiting evangelists would come, they would stand in the pulpit and say, "somebody been praying in this house." Prayer leaves a powerful residue. Although I have been gone from that church since 1997, they still have 9 am prayer. Every church I've attended, the Lord has allowed me to establish prayer, praise, and worship.

You would have thought everybody would be happy about prayer and the move of God, but I found out it was quite the contrary. A pastor from another faith came and got baptized. When his church found out he was reprimanded and removed. Others began to whisper and start rumors. It was hard to understand how something as powerful and simple as prayer would get people so worked up.

Because prayer is so powerful it brings out some things and reactions you don't expect. That's why earlier in this chapter I wrote about praying amiss. Some people have their own selfish desires, and some want attention. The enemy will come against your prayer life, but don't stop praying. I'm only telling you this so you are not blindsided and will know what to expect.

The Bible clearly tells us when Daniel prayed to the Lord that he ate no food, meat, or wine for three full weeks. He did not anoint himself with oil. Then a great vision came to Daniel and an angel told Daniel "Fear not Daniel for the first day you set thine heart to understand and to chasten thyself before thy God, thy words were heard." He said," I've come for your words, but the Prince of the kingdom of Persia withstood me for one and twenty days (21 days): but, lo, Michael, one of the chief princes, came to help me" (Daniel 10:12-14). The enemy will try to fight your prayer life with fear, confusion, disruption, and misunderstandings. Let me say this is a hard one. When you are praying and believing for a loved one who is sick to be healed and they die, it can take the wind out of you. The enemy comes to make you doubt and to stir up disbelief, but the same prayers that you prayed for your loved one, you will now have to pray for yourself. I'm a witness that your prayers will comfort you when you're looking for answers, to what you don't understand because you did everything that you knew to do, and the outcome goes another way. Some people say, "you don't question God" and I agree but, the Bible says we can ask and when we ask, He will comfort us like only He can with His word. I have had my prayers answered with the words "they are healed, just on the other side." I've also experienced the word of God comforting me saying "to be absent from the body is to be present with the Lord." Prayer and the word will keep your motives pure because we can ask, and He will answer us according to His word.

Let's go back to some things that will keep you from being distracted. Again, it is wise to set a prayer time. I like early in the morning because I like to invite Him into my day. I always ask

Him to go before me. Romans 8:27 says, "And he that searcheth the hearts knoweth what is the mind of the Spirit, because he maketh intercession for the saints according to the will of God." Now understand this, you should always have a praying spirit. There are times you may not have a specific prayer time, but for the most part you should plan it. Let our Heavenly Father know that He is first in your life. Give Him thanks and praise, acknowledge who He is. Cover yourself. Even on the airplane they advise passengers to put their mask on first before assisting anyone else. Ask Him for His divine assistance throughout your day. Ask Him to keep and protect your husband or wife, children, family, and your ministry, and those that work with you in ministry.

Being distracted can cost you. Here's an example. I made a promise to the Lord privately about a specific prayer time. I had a day when I didn't want to make good on my promise. No one else knew, but I knew. I blew the time, and I knew the difference in my day. Immediately my spirit said, "You didn't keep your word. Now things are disrupting your day." You feel uncovered like coming outside on a cold winter day in a bathing suit; not covered properly for the day. So, I went into my mode of split-second prayers.

Now let's talk about not praying your problem, but praying your solution. The reason I say to pray the solution is because you want victory. You want the answers. If you focus on the problem that's coming against you, you will begin to complain, get frustrated, not believe, doubt and cancel out your positive word results. The wrong words will cancel out your results. Your words and faith frame your world. Frames hold pictures. You will see what you say. You can pray the Psalm.

The Lord's prayer is considered the model prayer. "Our Father which art in heaven" means we acknowledge who He is and address Him as God, our Father. We acknowledge who He is and where He is. "Hallowed be thy name." His name is honored and holy above all. His name is great, mighty, and all-powerful. We tell Him of His worth. "Thy kingdom come thy will be done on earth as it is in heaven." God's way of doing things will be accomplished both on earth as in heaven. God provides for us and gives us what we need. "And forgive us our trespasses," means to ask for his forgiveness for sin both known and unknown to you. "As we forgive them that trespass against us." Forgive because you have been forgiven. "And lead us not into temptation but deliver us from evil." Keep the enemy away from us. He will put some space between you and the enemy. Then go back to praise. "For thine is the kingdom, the power, and the glory forever and ever. Amen."

For example, if you go to the doctor and find out you have a chronic disease, named cancer. Cancer has a name but, there is a name that is above all names. That name is Jesus! The Bible says, at that name every knee shall bow and every tongue confess. Philippians 2:9-11 says, "Wherefore God has highly exalted him and given him a name which is above every name. 10 That at the name of Jesus every knee shall bow of things in heaven and things in earth, and things under the earth." And that every tongue should confess that Jesus Christ is the Lord, to the glory of God the Father." So, cancer is a name. This is the prayer, "Father God, in the name of Jesus, your name is above the name cancer. So, cancer has to bow at the mighty name of Jesus. It is by Your stripes we were healed. I receive my healing." Then find the scriptures on healing.

You have to watch your words. Proverbs 18:21 says "death and life is in the power of the tongue and they that love it shall eat the fruit thereof." We have to stop saying "my cancer," "my kidney failure," and "my migraine." It's not yours and it is in direct violation for coming upon you. You have the power to feed or starve words. Words have power. One of the biggest lies ever told to us was "sticks and stones may break my bones, but words will never hurt me." Words can kill you and your emotions and tear down your self-esteem through verbal abuse. Words can also build you up. It is said that it takes five positive words to cancel out one negative word. Let's speak life. Instead of saying "my back is killing me," say "I thank God for a good, strong back." I think you get the point.

How to Pray With Understanding

Types of Prayer:

A prayer of invocation: to invite and invoke the presence of God. To ask, request and give permission to come. You acknowledge His awareness in this prayer. You're not asking for anything, just for Him to come and dwell with us. We welcome You here.

Prayer of petition and supplication: It is to ask what you desire and make your request known. This is where most of us spend our prayer time. Be careful to nothing, but in everything by prayer and supplication with thanksgiving make your request be made known unto God (Phil 4:6). We petition God; we ask and don't have to beg. He is our heavenly Father and wants to hear us talk to Him and tell him all about our situation and request. Sometimes its, "Lord, help me," "Lord, I need You," "Lord, show me, teach me." Ask God "why" and "what?" Speak from your heart.

They are your concerns so just pour it out. Don't stop there. Take some time out and be quiet to let the Holy Spirit speak to you. Prayer is communication. Communication requires speaking and listening. I quote one of the intercessors at Grace Church, "He is a master communicator."

Prayer of Intercession: seeking the Lord on behalf of others. Intercessory prayer is you standing in the gap for another, or others. God uses intercessors in many ways. For example, you have a person that comes on your mind, or comes to your spirit very strong and heavy; you just can't seem to shake that feeling or that person.

I remember having an urgent feeling to pray for my son. Well, actually it went like this. We were in a shut-in, all-night prayer. I was very tired. I told the other intercessors on the team I was going to pray, then I'm going in my office. When I got on my knees to pray the Holy Spirit came upon me to pray and speak life. It was very intense. My stomach was tight as I cried out to God for life. Oh, I remember saying "Live!" I was travailing and speaking in tongues until I felt a release about an hour or more later. Needless to say, the tiredness I felt when I came in was over. We prayed all night long. The next day we had a graduation party to attend as a family. It was a hot, hazy day. I took my mother with me who had dementia, and my three-year-old grandson. We were at the lake and all of a sudden, the hot, hazy day turned into a big storm off the lake. We all had to get out of the area. We had a baby screaming because he was afraid and a mother with dementia in a wheelchair, but we got to safety. Once we got settled at Mom's home safe, about three hours later my son, Ryan, came to the door to pick up his son. He began to hug and talk to his little son. He said, "You would have been so mad at Daddy." I looked at him and asked, "why?" He said, "Mom, we were out on the lake when that storm came up…on a small fishing boat. We called to the Coast Guard. It was bad. Something went wrong with the signal." He said, "We started east of the lighthouse and ended up six miles west, almost to Avon. It was a wild ride." He said they saw things people would not believe. Only God and intercession saved them. Remember, the night before we were in the shut in crying out to God for life. All of them made it to land safely. Oh yes, I will always give God praise for keeping them alive. Needless to say, the church carpet was on fire the next day from me praising God for saving my son and his friend's life!

Intercession is someone praying for you. I pray the intercessors not come down from their assignments until they are released by the Holy Spirit. What if I had just gone to my office and got some rest? We have a great intercessor according to Romans 8:26 NIV "In the same way the spirit helps us in our weaknesses, we do not know what we ought to pray for, but the Spirit himself intercedes for us through wordless groans. 27 And He who searches our hearts knows the mind of the Spirit." Intercede for God's people in accordance with the will of God.

Spiritual warfare prayer: warfare prayers hit bullseyes. You have a target and when you pray in the Spirit in your tongues (Heavenly language) you must be strategic when you come against the enemy. Sometimes we get angry with people, but it could be a spirit that is working through that person. So, try not to attack the person, but the spirit that's working through them. Identify the spirit, come against it, and send it back to the pits of hell to destroy, annihilate and cast it down. The enemy has an organized kingdom, but you have the power through prayer, the Word, and the Holy Spirit, to destroy it. Ephesians 6:2 says, "For wrestle not against flesh and blood but against principalities, against powers, against the rulers of darkness of this world. Against spiritual wickedness in high places." Rank and file.

Here is another powerful scripture. 2 Corinthians 10:4 says "the weapons of our warfare are not carnal, but mighty in God for pulling down strongholds. 5 Casting down imaginations and every high thing that exalts itself against the knowledge of God and bringing into captivity everything to the obedience of Christ. 6 And having in a readiness to revenge all disobedience." Warfare can require fasting with your prayers. Have high intense praise, then worship Him in victory.

Prayers of thanksgiving: All prayers should start and end with thanksgiving and praise. Enter into His gates with thanksgiving and into His courts with praise. Be thankful unto Him and bless His name (Psalm 100:4). Speak well of Him. Speak on His characteristics such as His love, goodness, kindness, and worth. Have a heart full of gratitude. When you have prayed about a job, healing, or anything else, just begin to tell Him "thank you." Say "Lord, I thank You for the job," "Lord, I thank You for my healing." Thank Him in advance. Think on His goodness. Clap your hands and let the tears flow, "Lord I just want to thank you!"

Take some time to write down your own prayers in the sections below.

PRAYERS OF INVOCATION

_____

_____

_____

_____

_____

_____

_____

_____

_____

_____

_____

_____

_____

_____

_____

_____

_____

_____

_____

_____

_____

_____

_____

_____

_____

_____

_____

_____

_____

_____

PRAYERS OF PETITION AND SUPPLICATION

_____

_____

_____

_____

_____

_____

_____

_____

_____

_____

_____

_____

_____

_____

_____

_____

_____

_____

_____

_____

_____

_____

_____

_____

_____

_____

_____

_____

_____

_____

_____

_____

_____

_____

_____

PRAYERS OF INTERCESSION

_____

_____

_____

_____

_____

_____

_____

_____

_____

_____

_____

_____

_____

_____

_____

_____

_____

_____

_____

_____

_____

_____

_____

_____

_____

_____

_____

_____

_____

_____

_____

_____

_____

Prayers of Spiritual Warfare

_____

_____

_____

_____

_____

_____

_____

_____

_____

_____

_____

_____

_____

_____

PRAYERS OF THANKSGIVING

_____

_____

_____

_____

_____

_____

_____

_____

_____

_____

_____

_____

_____

_____

_____

_____

_____

_____

_____

_____

_____

_____

_____

_____

_____

_____

_____

_____

_____

_____

_____

_____

_____

CHAPTER 5

How To Worship With Understanding

Worship that Moves God

Worship moves God when it is based on who God is. Ministering unto the Lord. What does that look like? We have to have daily practices unto the Lord. We have to have a daily prayer life, reading and daily devotions and meditating on His word. I see that statement over and over in the scriptures.

Daily devotions, reading, and meditating on his word. Let's look at some of the scriptures in the Bible so we can get the concept of God-centered worship that moves God.

Let's first look at the book of First Samuel. The main characters of this book are Samuel, Saul, and David. God's opposition to the proud, exaltation to the humble, faithful in spite of evil, and the promise of a messianic king. You can't talk about Samuel without first acknowledging his mother, Hannah and his father, Elkanah.

The book starts off with so much in the first twenty verses. It tells us who Elkanah was and where he came from. Elkanah had two wives, Hannah and Peninnah. Peninnah had children while Hannah had none. The story goes on to tell us year by year Elkanah would go to his city to worship and sacrifice to the Lord of Hosts at Shiloh. When Elkanah sacrificed, he would give portions to his wife Peninnah and all of their sons and daughters. He also gave to Hannah, but he would give her a double portion. Her womb was shut up and the other wife provoked her. When trouble came her way, she went to God at the altar. When she wept and did not eat, her husband would try to comfort her. He asked, "Am I not better than ten sons to you?" However, Hannah wanted her heart's desire. As she poured out at the altar, Eli, the priest, took notice of her. Keep in mind, your prayer will bring attention to you. Her prayer caused him to question her to see if she was drunk. Hannah was petitioning God for her son in detail. The Bible said she prayed with her heart, and although her lips moved, there was no sound. God can read your heart. She explained to the high priest, Eli that she was not drunk. He actually came into agreement with her and confirmed God would open her womb. Time passed and she received what she asked of the Lord, her son, Samuel. Hannah kept her vow she made to the Lord that after he was born, she would give him back to the Lord (in his youth). I just wanted to give that history so we can see sacrificial worship to God. Samuel grew and ministered to the Lord with obedience and honor day after day. Can you give your answered prayer back to God or is it only for your own self-reward and pleasure? That worship moved God and the word says He opened her womb, and she had three more sons and two daughters.

That worship moved God to move on her behalf. That very act of worship caused God's hand to move. Let's look at what that worship consisted of: heart felt prayers, obedience, faithfulness in spite of evil (God's opposition to the proud and exaltation of the humble).

Here is Hannah's prayer of thanks in 1 Sam 2:1-10 (KJV)

And Hannah prayed, and said, My heart rejoiceth in the LORD: mine horn is exalted in the Lord: my mouth is enlarged over mine enemies; because I rejoice in thy salvation.

2   *There is* none holy as the LORD: for *there is* none beside thee: neither *is there* any rock like our God.

3   Talk no more so exceeding proudly; let *not* arrogancy come out of your mouth: for the LORD *is* a God of knowledge, and by him actions are weighed.

4   The bows of the mighty men *are* broken, and they that stumbled are girded with strength.

5   *They that were* full have hired out themselves for bread; and *they that were* hungry ceased: so that the barren hath born seven; and she that hath many children is waxed feeble.

6   The LORD killeth, and maketh alive: he bringeth down to the grave, and bringeth up.

7   The LORD maketh poor, and maketh rich: he bringeth low, and lifteth up.

8   He raiseth up the poor out of the dust, *and* lifteth up the beggar from the dunghill, to set *them* among princes, and to make them inherit the throne of glory: for the pillars of the earth *are* the LORD'S, and he hath set the world upon them.

9   He will keep the feet of his saints, and the wicked shall be silent in darkness; for by strength shall no man prevail.

10   The adversaries of the LORD shall be broken to pieces; out of heaven shall he thunder upon them: the LORD shall judge the ends of the earth; and he shall give strength unto his king, and exalt the horn of his anointed.

I can't say this enough, daily practices, a life of obedience, faith, and being humble is worship that moves God.

Now let's look at the tabernacle of Moses. This lets us know we have access directly to the throne of God. In the Old Testament, only the high priest could enter into the Holy of Holies.

I will enter His gates. The first place in the tabernacle was the opening gates. Entering the gates means you have entered into a relationship with God. The word tabernacle means to dwell. It speaks of God's desire to dwell with His people. God always desires to make himself accessible to man. Man cannot approach God any way he wants to. He can approach God through the provided way. Jesus calls himself "The Door." The gate of the tabernacle was the only way to enter. It was wide and inviting. Nevertheless, it was the only entrance. In the same way, our entrance in relationship with God is always, and only, through Jesus Christ. Enter at the gate.

I'd like to take this time to offer Christ to you as your personal savior. This is the beginning of it all. "Confess Him with your mouth, believe in your heart that God has raised Him from the dead, thou shall be saved. For with the heart man believeth unto righteousness and with the mouth confession is made unto salvation" (Romans 10:9-10). God dwells in place and now He dwells in people.

Once a year the high priest would go in and make atonement for the people. He could not have any sin in his life. He would wear bells and pomegranates tied to the bottom of his robe, and a rope tied about his waist. The priest had to be clean to enter. He would fall dead if he had any sin in his life. When this happened, the people would pull him out by the rope that was tied about him. The bells ringing on the bottom of the robe was an indication he was still alive to make sacrifices. That was the job of the high priest. We thank God for Jesus because he was without sin.

At the entrance of the tabernacle was the brazen, or bronze, altar. That's the first place we need to take ourselves. That's where the flesh was burned. Think of that as your place of pouring out, not holding back anything. You are the sacrifice. It was animal sacrifice, but you are the sacrifice on the altar.

The bronze altar had a two-fold ministry, consecration, and atonement. As seen in the types of offerings given there, each of those has application to us in our walk with the Lord. As you look at your own heart, ask God to bring to mind any offenses against Him that are unresolved. Have you offended Him through disobedient acts directly or indirectly?

Then consecration speaks of dedication. Though the burnt offerings dealt with sin, consecrations main purpose was one of indicating a life devoted to God. The most important thing to place on the altar is ourselves. Have you dedicated yourself to the Lord?

Now we are at the bronze laver. While the altar teaches us about the ministry of reconciliation, the laver speaks of the ministry of sanctification. It does an initial cleansing and a continual cleansing.

It is important that I tell you what it was made of. It was made of brass. It has been said they asked the women to bring their mirrors to construct the bronze laver. One of the revelations I received as I was teaching worship at the church, was as you wash in the laver with the water, you could begin to see a reflection of yourself and observe how much more you needed to look like God.

As we walk the way of the priest, we must remind ourselves that we too are priests. 1 Peter 2:9 teaches us we are a "royal priesthood." Each of us as New Testament believers can walk the way of the Old Testament priests.

Say this prayer, "Father God, in the name of Jesus, I come to You asking You for forgiveness of sins (name them), known and unknown to me. I acknowledge that I need You as savior over my life. I give You every part of me. You have my heart, my mind, and my soul. I desire to walk with You and to obey Your word. In Jesus' name, amen."

Next is the golden lampstand. The lampstand was made from one talon of pure gold. Gold was the most precious metal of that day. It's melting process speaks of purity. The lampstand had seven lamps. One central branch and three branches on each side. The golden lampstand would be the first item to catch the eye of the worshiper as he entered into the Holy Place. It provided the only light inside of the tent. It was a continual reminder that where God dwells there is light. Jesus is the light of the world. Jesus' light gives direction and draws men to the Father and eternal life.

Leviticus 24:1-4 teaches that it was the duty of the priests to keep the wick trimmed and maintained so that the light of the lamps would never dim. The obvious application here is the need for each of us to attend to our light, that we might always be a witness.

The table of the bread of presence (show bread) speaks of God as the sustenance and satisfaction to His people. Food speaks of fellowship. The table reminds us that God is continually waiting for fellowship with us. The bread was placed regularly before the Lord, but the priest actually consumed it. It is a picture of God's provision. God will provide. I hope you are getting the concept of worship according to the dwelling place of God.

Jesus said, "I am the bread of life." It is important to remember the sweet fellowship with God is only possible for those who have first experienced forgiveness and consecration at the altar, being cleansed with the symbolic laver. There is no other way to enter into the presence of God and enjoy Him. Once we have entered the Holy Place in the proper way, we can partake of this bread of life. Remember, food (bread) is satisfying but, it is also sustaining. Physically when it comes to living healthy lives, food consumption is not an option. Likewise, we spiritually stand in daily need of the bread of God lest we die in our ability to worship.

Say this prayer, "Father, we thank You that You are the light. The light that ends darkness. We look to You for direction, peace, love, and strength. Show us the way that we may walk in the light of You each and every day that we may also be a light shining in darkness."

The altar of incense. The incense altar set in front of the veil into the Holy of Holies. The altar sitting as it did, just outside the Holy of Holies, was as close as one could get to God. It was a place of prayer. Prayer will get you close to God. It is the fire that burns continuously at this altar. A Holy place. The altar of incense is a reminder of the role prayer plays in the life of a believer. If our hearts are clean, every time you and I lift our voices toward heaven to speak to the Lord, our prayers are like fragrant aromas rising to the Father. Prayer is key.

Then there's the veil. The veil was a heavy curtain that closed off the most Holy Place. The historian, Josephus wrote that it was as thick as a hand's breadth (four inches) and that a team of horses pulling in each direction could not tear it. The purpose for the veil was to serve as a partition between the Holy Place and the Holy of Holies where the ark of the covenant was kept. The veil is spoken of in the New Testament at the moment Jesus breathed his last breath the veil was torn in two from top to bottom (Matthew 27:51). The New Testament believer can enter the very presence of God through the veil by the blood of Jesus. The veil is called his flesh. What a contrast to the Old Testament where only the high priest could enter once a year at the day of atonement. The veil, we are told, is a picture of Jesus' body sacrifice for us. When the veil was torn in two, it painted a visual reminder of the ideal covenant. When we walk this path, we have access to the Holy of Holies through Jesus Christ. There is no more separation.

Keep on coming with me. We are in a place of worship.

Next is the ark of the covenant and mercy seat. The ark of the covenant is none other than the throne of God. It was covered by the mercy seat and two cherubim made of pure gold. It was the holiest of all the furniture. Primarily it points to the necessity of doing things God's way. It was to be carried by the priest. Inside the ark was a golden jar holding the manna; a reminder of God's faithful provision in the wilderness, Aaron's rod which budded (a reminder of God's affirmation of the priesthood), and the tables of the covenant (a reminder of Israel's accountability to God's laws as part of his covenant with God). Like the ark, we cannot handle God any kind of way. We have been given specific instructions on how to approach God's throne.

You have followed the path of the priest. You have gone from outside the gate, past the brazen altar, and the laver into the Holy Place with the lampstand and table of show bread. You have passed the altar of incense and have gone through the veil into the very presence of God. You have gazed at his throne and experienced the wonder of the angels and His mercy. You have worshiped.

So, position yourself to minister to the Lord in your worship. It's a lifestyle. Yes, let the music move you to worship the Lord. Dr Dwayne Hardin said, "Worship is more about alignment with God for the fulfilment of purpose rather than hands in the air and the slow song, minus substance." Music moves me. Worship moves God.

Let's posture ourselves for true worship. The scripture says, "to present yourself as a living sacrifice, holy and acceptable unto God which is your reasonable service" (Romans 12:1). The spirit of the Lord is calling us back to true worship. Align yourself. John 4:24 says "For God is a spirit. And those that worship Him, must worship Him in spirit and in truth." From your heart to God's ears, let's worship Him. Let's continue to grow and develop. God dwells in places and now he dwells in people. The Tabernacle represents the body. It says in 1 Corinthians 6:19, "What? Know ye not that your body is the temple of the Holy Ghost, which is in you, which ye have of God, and ye are not your own". The Tabernacle was a movable structure where God dwelt among His people, the Temple was a permanent structure, but your body is the permanent structure now.

There were three different compartments in the Tabernacle. Three (3) represents fullness. Past, Present, Future – Outer Court, Inner Court, Holy of Holies – Body, Soul, Spirit, - Father, Son, Holy Ghost. Thanksgiving, Praise, and Worship. When people want to have an experience of God, they come with a thanks offering and offer it in the outer court and expect God to bless them Micah 6:6 says, Wherewith shall I come before the Lord, and bow myself before the high God? shall I come before him with burnt offerings, with calves of a year old?". Enter into His gates with thanksgiving. Sadly, many people are satisfied with just an outer court level. Romans 12:1 says, I beseech you therefore brethren, by the mercies of God, that ye present your bodies as a living sacrifice, holy, acceptable unto God, which is your reasonable service.

Application and Discussion

Let's use this space to discuss further the life of Samuel's duties in the temple. After reading about Samuel's life in your Bible, use the space below to write down what Samuel did in each phase of his life. Reflect on your own growth as well.

Samuel Grew

_____

_____

_____

_____

_____

_____

Eli knew the voice of the Lord

_____

_____

_____

_____

_____

_____

_____

_____

_____

_____

_____

_____

_____

_____

_____

_____

_____

_____

_____

_____

_____

_____

_____

_____

_____

_____

_____

_____

_____

_____

_____

ELI TAUGHT SAMUEL HOW TO HEAR

God used Samuel before he knew the voice of God. When Samuel heard the voice of God, Samuel did not know what he was hearing. It took Eli to clarify whose voice it was. Eli instructed Samuel to say the next time he heard the voice, "Speak Lord, for your servant is here" 1 Samuel 3:9. What three things did Samuel learn about listening?

SAMUEL TOLD ELI WHAT GOD SAID

_____

_____

_____

_____

_____

_____

_____

_____

_____

_____

_____

_____

_____

_____

_____

How do we listen to hear the voice of God? People hear in different ways. Discuss below ways people hear God's voice.

_____

_____

_____

_____

_____

_____

_____

_____

_____

_____

_____

_____

_____

This book is a great tool to take you into deeper studies on Worship that pleases God. Divinely inspiring, this dynamic guide has been made available for training praise and worship teams, worship leaders, and ministry. You won't be disappointed with the move of God.

Made in the USA
Middletown, DE
05 March 2023

26158776R00060